On the Road Again!

On the Road Again!

MORE TRAVELS WITH MY FAMILY

BY *Marie-Louise Gay*
AND *David Homel*

GROUNDWOOD BOOKS
HOUSE OF ANANSI PRESS
TORONTO BERKELEY

Groundwood Books / House of Anansi Press
110 Spadina Avenue, Suite 801, Toronto, Ontario M5V 2K4
or c/o Publishers Group West
1700 Fourth Street, Berkeley CA 94710

We acknowledge for their financial support of our publishing program the
Canada Council for the Arts, the Government of Canada through the
Canada Book Fund (CBF) and the Ontario Arts Council.

 Canada Council
for the Arts
Conseil des Arts
du Canada
 ONTARIO ARTS COUNCIL
CONSEIL DES ARTS DE L'ONTARIO

Library and Archives Canada Cataloguing in Publication
Gay, Marie-Louise
On the road again! : more travels with my
family / by Marie-Louise Gay and David Homel.
ISBN 978-1-55498-087-1
I. Homel, David II. Title.
PS8563.A868O52 2011   jC813'.54   C2010-904468-1

Design by Michael Solomon
Printed and bound in Canada

To our friends and neighbors in Celeriac

My Adventures

The big surprise

"Guess what, Charlie?" yelled my brother as he burst into my bedroom.

He was wearing his plaid Sherlock Holmes cap with the flaps, and he was clutching a magnifying glass in his hand.

"Hmm… Let's see," I said. "You've been spying on Mom and Dad."

"How did you know?"

"Elementary, my dear Watson."

Max shrugged. He had no idea what I was talking about. He had never actually read *The Adventures of Sherlock Holmes*. He'd only looked at the pictures.

"You'll never guess where we're going on our next trip."

And before I could answer, he shouted, "France! That's right, *Vee ahre goink to Frahnce.*"

He put on his Pink Panther fake French accent. He always mixes up the Pink Panther and Sherlock Holmes. What a knucklehead!

That was some pretty exciting news. I'd always dreamed of going to Paris. I'd even made a list of the things I wanted to see.

First off was the Eiffel Tower, of course. No elevator for me. I'd climb every one of the 1,665 steps to the very top and see the whole city at my feet. Then I wanted to look at the spot where the Hunchback of Notre Dame took the plunge.

Next on my list was the underground stuff: the metro that was a hundred times bigger than Montreal's subway system, and a boat ride through the sewers of Paris. They both probably smelled about the same. And I'd read somewhere that you could visit caves under the city where the Romans used to bury their dead. You could see huge piles of skulls and bones by candlelight! Try and picture that!

Not to mention the French Disneyland. That's right. There is a French version of Disneyland not far from Paris. I wondered if Mickey Mouse wore a beret and carried a loaf of French bread under his arm. I couldn't wait to find out.

We went into the living room where my parents were studying a gigantic map of France. It looked as if every little village and stream and castle was marked on this map of theirs. Maybe even every mushroom!

And that was how I found out that we were not going to Paris after all. My mother had her finger on the name of a village that was smaller than a speck of dust, somewhere in the hills in the southern part of France. When she took her finger off the dot, I read the name of the village.

It was called Celeriac. *Sell-air-ee-ack*. I think that's some kind of a vegetable. Imagine coming from a village that's named after a vegetable. And not even a famous one either!

"We have a big surprise for you," she announced.

My brother and I looked at each other. Our parents' surprises usually mean bad news for us. Like the time we nearly died in a sandstorm in the middle of the Arizona desert because they didn't want to go to a normal place like the Grand Canyon. Or that little picnic we had with the alligators in some swamp whose name I still can't pronounce.

"We're going to live in Celeriac for a year," my mother told us. "We found a lovely old house that's walking distance from your new school. And the countryside is breathtaking. Isn't that wonderful?"

My brother and I stared at her. Was my mother going crazy? A year in France?

"It's going to be a real cultural experience," my father chimed in. "They have a great civilization there."

He started reeling off all the different cultural attractions we were going to enjoy. Let's see... There would be castles and plenty of ruins, courtesy of the Romans, but without any skulls and piles of bones. Pieces of aqueducts, oppidums and all sorts of other things I had never heard of.

My father went on and on. The trip was going to be like *Asterix*, but without the jokes. Or like a year-long history class without recess.

I looked at my parents. They were smiling away.

But I couldn't believe it! They had secretly planned the whole trip without even talking about it with me. I didn't want to leave my friends, my school and my neighborhood. I didn't want to spend a year in a tiny village named after a vegetable, hidden away in the mountains somewhere.

How come parents think they can just decide for you? It's not fair!

And that's exactly what I told them.

"You'll make new friends,"

my mother said. "You're good at that. It will be an incredible experience. I'm sure it will change your life."

"I like my life just the way it is."

"You'll remember the trip for years to come," my mother went on.

"You mean I'll have nightmares every night?"

"You'll see, Charlie," my father said. "It'll be a great adventure. And we'll be back before you know it. You'll have some great stories to tell your friends."

I hated to admit it, but he did have a point. My friends were always pretty impressed by my travel adventures.

In the end, I made a deal with my parents. After our year in the village, we would go to Paris and see everything on my list.

My little brother started jumping up and down like a frog. He grabbed Miro, our cat.

"Miro," he yelled. "Guess what? We're going to France!"

I saw my parents look at each other.

Then I understood. Miro wasn't coming with us.

ONE

We lose my brother on the airplane

S o there we were on the day of our departure, at the beginning of an incredible adventure, as my mother would say, but we were too disorganized to get out of the house. As usual, my family made a big embarrassing show for the whole neighborhood.

First, Miro decided to hide. He didn't want to leave home either. My mother and I walked around the house and up and down the alleyway, calling his name. Finally I discovered him underneath the front porch. I crawled under and grabbed him. But Miro can be really stubborn sometimes. He dug in his paws and refused to budge. When I finally managed to drag him from under the porch, we were both muddy and covered in cobwebs. I had to change my clothes while my mother dusted off Miro.

Then my brother started to cry because he didn't want to leave Miro, even though our cat was going to be happy staying at my grandmother's house. Better than chasing French mice in some backward mountain village! He would be treated like a king at my grandmother's. Round-the-clock food! All the petting he wanted! He would be enormous by the time we came back.

Our friends who were taking us to the airport were parked outside, honking their horn and pointing at their watches. That's because my father kept rushing back into the house because he forgot something.

The first time, it was his glasses. The second time, it was his typewriter and all the notes for the book he was supposed to be writing in France. Believe it or not, my father still uses a typewriter!

We were finally on our way when my brother realized he'd forgotten his penguin. So we rushed back inside again. Our friends must have wished they'd never offered to drive us to the airport.

My mother was looking more and more frazzled.

"That's enough!" she yelled. "You've got one minute to find that penguin, or we'll leave without it!"

My mother's the kind of person who likes to be at the airport early, hours before the plane leaves. That wasn't going to happen today.

Of course, I found the penguin, under Max's bed. Then we rushed back to the car.

After we checked our baggage, my father gave us a long speech about how we had to be serious at the security gate. We weren't supposed to say words like "gun" or "bomb," or make jokes about hijacking the airplane.

At the X-ray machine, the guards made my father take off his cowboy boots. I suppose a man who doesn't look anything like a cowboy and who is wearing cowboy boots seems suspicious. I knew it — there were holes in both his socks.

The security guard picked up my brother's stuffed penguin and poked it in the stomach.

"Hmm… This penguin looks rather fat. Are you sure you didn't hide anything in it?"

Was that a joke? From the security guard's expression, I couldn't tell. That must be the first thing you learn in security guard school: how to keep a poker face, no matter what.

My brother looked very insulted. He grabbed

the penguin from the guard's hand and marched right past the metal detector, toward our gate. Good thing he didn't have any metal in his pockets.

"Wait!" my father called, struggling to get his boots back on.

"Go and catch up to him," my mother ordered me. "Don't let him get lost."

It was starting already. I was going to have to look after my brother, as usual.

I found him standing in front of the window of the duty-free store, looking at all the electronic stuff for sale, cameras and iPods and watches. He still looked insulted.

"They let your penguin through, didn't they? So what's the matter?"

"That man said he was fat!"

And he went on staring at the gadgets in the window. My brother is so touchy about his penguin.

But we weren't through arguing with the people who worked at the airport. When I looked up, I saw my mother trying to convince the man at the gate that her enormous portfolio with all her drawings inside would fit on the plane. The man was shaking his head No. My mother was nodding her head Yes. Everyone was staring at her, since she was holding up the line. To make matters worse, my father joined the conversation, too.

I just stared at the gadgets in the store window and pretended that I didn't know these people. Sometimes parents are just too embarrassing.

My mother and the man ended up compromising. My mother could take her portfolio on the plane. But it would have to go in a special closet where the crew kept their bags. That was good enough for her.

Once we boarded the plane, my father kept telling us not to be scared, and how safe air travel is. I didn't understand what he was talking about. Then I figured out that he was the one who was scared, because right away he took a sleeping pill. As the plane took off, my father sat rigid, staring straight ahead, hardly breathing at all. He finally relaxed a little when we reached our cruising altitude.

But the pill sure worked fast! In no time he was snoring away with his mouth open.

"Don't bother him," my mother told us. "After we land, he has to drive all day to Celeriac."

She didn't look very happy, maybe because she was squished in next to my brother and me. No chance of her falling asleep!

We had been on airplanes before, but never on one this huge, and with so much free stuff. My brother started exploring the big pocket in the seat in front of him. He opened the "For Your

Comfort" bag and took out everything. He put on the pair of socks. He wanted to brush his teeth with the toothbrush that already had toothpaste on it, but my mother told him to wait until after dinner. He put on the sleeping mask and pretended to be a robber, which didn't make much sense, since how can you be a robber if you can't see anything?

Then he started playing with the telephone that was on the back of the seat in front of him.

"I'm going to call Grandma," he announced.

I knew you needed a credit card to make the phone work, so there was no danger of that happening. I started reading the in-flight magazine. It had all kinds of information about the plane we were on.

Then I heard my brother talking. I figured he was just pretending to talk to Grandma, fooling around the way he always does. The next thing I knew, he started meowing, which is how he talks to Miro.

Then he hung up the phone.

"Grandma says Miro is just fine," he said. "But Miro says he misses us already."

I took the phone from the seat back. I couldn't hear anything.

"It worked for me," my brother said proudly. "You have to say the secret password."

"Oh, yeah? What's that?"

"Hello," he said.

Another one of his jokes! But then I heard Grandma on the other end of the line, talking to the cat, and Miro meowing back. Then she hung up.

I'll never understand how he did it. It must cost a fortune to talk on the phone in an airplane when you're a million kilometers above the earth. Talk about long distance!

Though the plane was enormous, everything in it was very small. A tiny meal arrived on a tiny tray. On the tray were miniature packets of salt and pepper. The knives and forks were made for elves, and those elves could have used the tiny ketchup containers for their elf French fries.

Not to mention the bathrooms. They were smaller than my closet at home. You could sit on the toilet and wash your face in the sink at the same time, as I soon found out.

After the meal, I got out *Silverwing*, the book I was reading. Ever since I saw millions of bats flying out of a cave at nightfall from the Carlsbad Caverns, I've wanted to learn everything I can about them. The book is incredible. The author must have been a bat in another life. Otherwise, how could he know what bats think and feel?

My mother was reading to my brother. He had brought *Chicken Little* with him. The two of them were squeaking, "The sky is falling! The sky is falling!"

I really didn't think that was a good choice for a story, since we were actually *in* the sky. The passenger on the other side of the row thought the same way I did. He kept shooting little looks at my mother.

My brother gets bored quickly. He didn't want to read any more. He wanted to bother my mother. And he's very good at it. He kept asking when we were going to get to France, and how come the time was different there, and how was it that something as heavy as an airplane could stay up in the sky.

Finally, my mother got so tired of him that she told me to take him to see the pilot.

"How do you know they'll let us in the cockpit?"

"You're kids," she said. "They always let kids do that. Now just go."

We had to pass through First Class to reach the cockpit. That's the section of the plane where the seats are bigger, and where there is even more stuff in the "For Your Comfort" bag. You get more pillows, and champagne instead of apple juice in a box.

"I wouldn't mind sitting up here," my brother said.

A flight attendant stopped us.

"And where are you boys headed?" she asked.

"We want to see the cockpit," my brother announced loudly.

"Really? Are you going to fly the plane?"

She must have told that joke a hundred times.

"Computers fly the plane," I told her. "Everybody knows that."

"Well, you can tell that to the pilots and see what they say," she laughed.

When we entered the cockpit with the flight attendant behind us, both the pilot and the co-pilot were eating their dinners, which does prove that computers really do fly the plane. I was surprised to see they had the same food we did. I was sure they would be eating something better.

They stopped eating and showed us the throttle — they called it the joystick. Then we saw the radar screen, the speedometer, the altimeter that tells you how high you are and all sorts of other things.

My brother was so impressed he didn't even say anything. And that's pretty rare.

Then the pilot pulled on a metal handle that was hanging from the ceiling. A weird vibrating sound started up that was pretty loud. My brother jumped and hit his head on the fire extinguisher.

"Don't worry!" the pilot laughed. "We're just starting up the lawn mower. It's time to cut the grass."

My brother looked around, rubbing his head. He didn't know what to think.

"That's the warning signal," the co-pilot said, "for when we're losing altitude. But don't worry. My colleague was just playing tricks on you. He's always doing that. Imagine if you were his kids!"

"I wish my father was a pilot," my brother said. Then he looked at me. "Don't tell Dad that, okay?"

The pilots laughed. Then the flight attendant told us it was time to let the pilots do their job, which was to eat their dinner off a plastic tray.

"Back already?" my mother asked. She looked as if she'd been sleeping.

I plugged in my earphones. *Spaceballs* was playing. I love that movie. My brother didn't want to watch it because he'd seen it already. So had I, at least seven times, but that didn't bother me.

"Why don't you go for a walk?" my mother told him, yawning.

He climbed out of his seat, crawled across my lap, made sure he stepped on my toes, then began running up and down the aisles. He sure made a lot of friends that way, especially with the flight attendants who were trying to push their carts. I concentrated on the movie and pretended he wasn't my brother.

I must have slept for a while, because when I opened my eyes, the movie was over and the plane was dark. Everyone was sleeping.

That's when my mother woke up with a start.

"Where's Max?" she asked.

"I don't know." I yawned a couple of times. "You told him to go for a walk."

Suddenly she was worried. That's just like her. First she tells my brother to take a walk, and when he does, she gets all nervous because she doesn't know exactly where he is.

She got up and started walking down the aisles. Then she tried the bathrooms – all of them.

I know my brother better than that. He wouldn't hide in a bathroom the size of a peanut. Especially not a stinky peanut.

Next thing I knew, she was talking to one of the flight attendants. A minute later, there was a very loud announcement over the loudspeaker system that woke everyone up.

"If anyone has seen a small boy with blond hair, holding a stuffed penguin, please inform the nearest flight attendant. His name is Max. The boy's name, that is. Not the penguin's."

I didn't understand what all the fuss was about. After all, people can't get lost in an airplane, can they? Max wasn't about to open the door and go for a stroll, was he? He was probably just playing tricks on us, as usual.

When my mother came back, she still looked worried. I could feel her trying to be logical, but not really succeeding.

Suddenly I had an idea. I unplugged my earphones and put down my book and went to the first-class section of the plane with the big comfortable seats.

A blanket was spread out on one of them. From under the blanket, a pink webbed foot was sticking out.

A penguin foot.

Under the blanket, Max was stretched out, sleeping away without a care in the world.

I went back and told my mother, but she didn't believe me. She had to go and see for herself.

My father was sleeping. My brother was sleeping. It was my turn now.

A short time later, I opened my eyes and looked out the window. The sunlight was blinding. Far below, I saw tiny purple and green and yellow squares. Those were fields, and the white dots in them were sheep. In the middle of the fields was a miniature pink castle with real turrets.

In just a few hours, we had gone from night in Montreal to a bright sunny morning in France.

I wondered where the night went. It could have fallen into one of those black holes in outer space that you hear about.

Then I had the craziest thought. My mother had explained to me that tomorrow would come faster because we were flying to Europe. But let's say that we kept on flying. Would we grow up sooner, since we were rushing so quickly into the future? I wondered if I could ever get back the hours I'd lost over the Atlantic Ocean, or whether they were gone forever.

It was just like time travel in a science fiction story. I guess that was part of the "incredible adventure" my parents had promised.

TWO

A duck thief on the loose!

A s we crossed the old stone bridge into the village where we were going to live, the first thing we saw was a robbery. And it was happening in broad daylight.

"Look!" Max pointed. "That guy has a duck under his coat."

Sure enough, a grizzled old man was climbing up from the riverbank below. He was trying to hide a large white duck under his long coat that looked totally out of place in summer. The duck didn't like it under the man's coat, so it would poke its head out every few seconds. And quack, very loudly.

"Don't look," my mother told us. "And don't point. I bet that man is stealing the duck from the river. I'm sure that's illegal."

"Shouldn't we call the police?" I asked.

"Normally we would, but in a foreign country, sometimes it's better to mind your own business until you get to know how things work," my mother answered.

"Anyway, the police probably steal ducks, too," my father laughed.

Duck-stealing police? What kind of place was this?

The man passed us. He was looking straight ahead, and acting as if everyone walked around the village with ducks under their coats.

The duck quacked again, twice as loud. All the ducks along the river quacked back. The man walked just a little bit faster, then disappeared into a narrow alley between two houses.

The duck thief had made his getaway in plain sight!

"I want a pet duck," my brother said, looking down at the river. "They're cute."

"He didn't steal that duck for a pet," I told him.

Max looked at me. "Then why did he take it?"

My mother shot me one of her warning looks. I decided I'd better keep quiet.

The house we were going to live in that year stood on a tiny street just wide enough for one car to squeeze through. And not just any car. More like the one we had, a Renault 4L, a miniature station wagon that looked like a sardine can on wheels. There were no sidewalks, so when a car came down our street, it practically scratched the walls of our house. Which is why hardly any of the cars in the village had side-view mirrors.

But it turned out there wasn't much traffic, and I discovered why the very first day. In the middle of the street lay a fat old dog. Was it sleeping... or dead?

I saw it twitch its ears once. Not dead.

I wondered what would happen if a car came

along, and I soon found out. The dog didn't move a muscle. When the driver saw it, he didn't bother honking his horn. He just stopped, backed up and drove away.

If you were a dog, this was the town for you!

The old lady from across the street opened her door and set down a bowl.

"Linda!" she called. "*Viens manger!*"

The dog — or Linda, I should say — slowly got up, yawned and shuffled over to the door, where she started gobbling down her lunch. What a tough life!

"Her name is Linda?" my brother asked.

"Yes. Linda means 'pretty' in Spanish," said our neighbor, who was called Madame Mendes, judging from the name on her mailbox.

Pretty? Linda was the ugliest dog I'd ever seen. She was fat and wrinkled and had large brownish liver spots.

But she did make an excellent speed bump.

I'm going to tell you a few things about our house, and I hope you'll believe me.

Our house was like nothing else I'd ever seen. The downstairs had an enormous fireplace big enough to park a car in. A sardine-can car, that is.

A stone trough stood beside our dining table, and a round opening in the floor that had been closed with a concrete cover showed where a well had been.

"In the old days, the animals lived on the ground floor," my father explained. "The people got their water from their own well. They lived upstairs, and the heat rising from the animals helped keep them warm."

Later that winter, as I shivered under a hundred layers of blankets, I wished we had a few cows and horses downstairs to keep our house warm.

We ran up the enormous stone staircase that led to the two top floors. Everything was made out of stone, including the walls. The rooms were huge. The bathroom had a bathtub the size of a swimming pool. Once upon a time, a giant must have lived here.

Behind the house was the *jardin*, as the French call it, but it was really just a tiny patch of ground with a scruffy old palm tree growing in the middle. There wasn't even enough room to kick a soccer ball around.

My brother and I went to the front of the house where our rooms were. We threw open the shutters. We knew how narrow the street was, but still, it was a little strange to look out the window and see right into the house across the way.

And guess who was there? Madame Mendes.

She and her husband were eating lunch. We could even see what they were having: fried fish. Two fishes each.

Madame Mendes and her husband turned and waved.

"I guess we're going to get to know the neighbors pretty well," my brother said, waving back.

"I hope you like the smell of fried fish," I told him, "since this is your room."

"How come I get the smaller one?"

"Because you're smaller. Why else?"

We decided to go exploring. We left the house and quickly discovered that the village ended with our narrow street. We walked past a field with horses busy eating grass. Then we came to two cemeteries separated by a vineyard where fat purple grapes were growing. In front of the cemeteries were benches crowded with people.

Everyone turned and stared at us.

"I don't know about this place," my brother said. "I don't think we'll ever fit in here."

"How come?"

"Look at them. Everybody's really old."

He was right. Our parents were pretty old, but nothing like these people. They looked as if they were at least a hundred, though with old people it's kind of hard to tell. I wondered if this was the line-up to get into the cemetery.

"How come there are two cemeteries?" my brother wanted to know.

There was only one way to find out. I walked up to one of the old ladies sitting on a bench.

"Excuse me, but why are there two cemeteries right beside each other?"

"What did you say there, young man?"

The old woman leaned forward and cupped her hand to her ear. Either she was deaf, or she didn't understand me. My father had told us that people in France might not understand our accent. Well, their accent was pretty hard to understand, too.

"How come you've got two cemeteries here?" I shouted into the lady's ear.

The old woman yelled to an even older lady on the bench right next to her, "I can't understand what this nice young man is saying."

"That's because you're as deaf as a doorknob," the lady yelled back.

I looked at my brother and tried not to laugh. Our parents had also warned us that we would have to be very polite in France. But I guess it depended on how old you were. The older you were, the ruder you could be.

Finally, a red-faced man answered, "One cemetery is for the Catholics. The other is for the Protestants."

"Oh," I said. "I see."

But I didn't see at all. The two cemeteries seemed exactly the same to me.

"But underneath it all, they're friends again," the man told us.

I wondered what he meant. How could you be friends with someone under the ground?

"That vineyard was planted here so they can drink together. Just because they're dead doesn't mean they can't have a nice glass of red wine!" the man chortled.

As he laughed, his face turned purple, the same color as the grapes. I bet he had drunk a bit of that nice red wine himself.

That was one of the first things I learned about Celeriac, our speck-of-dust village. Wine was very important to the people here. Some of them even drank it for breakfast.

That made sense, I suppose, because growing grapes was what most people in the village did for a living.

Next, our explorations led us to the center of the village. Actually, our noses led us there, because we smelled the open-air market before we saw it. Boy, did they eat some strange things in this place!

First, I spotted a mean-looking swordfish, sword and all, displayed on a bed of bloody ice. But the fish-seller had more than just fish. There were all sorts of seashells, the kind you might collect on the beach, but you'd never think of eating whatever lives inside.

He also had some strange sea-insects called *cigales de mer* that were still alive. They looked like creatures from outer space with their long antennae. Their sharp claws waved at me, as if warning me to stay away. But a lady stepped up and bought every last one of them. She dropped them into her straw shopping basket, where they immediately started making plans to escape.

Next to the fish-seller was a lady who sold cheeses. Very moldy cheeses. You couldn't miss her. You just had to take a deep breath! Phew!

One man had rabbits hanging by their feet, with the fur still on them. Another guy wearing a straw hat was giving away free slices of sausage.

Of course my brother made a beeline in his direction.

"*Bon appétit!*" the man said, and he cut a slice of sausage for him with a very sharp knife.

My brother munched away, then asked for another one.

"You like it, do you?"

"Uh-huh," Max said with his mouth full.

"It's donkey sausage," the man told him. "Grade A, the very best. From donkeys I raised myself."

My brother turned red. Then green. Then he swallowed hard.

"Hee-haw, hee-haw!" I brayed into his ear.

He chased me down the street. But it was pretty hard to run on a street crowded with people. We stopped in front of a stall that had dead pigs trussed up for everyone to admire.

"Those pigs are making faces at us," my brother claimed.

"Imagine if someone sliced you open from your bellybutton to your throat," I told him. "You'd make a face, too."

A half-dozen cooked pig heads were lined up on the counter. They all had their tongues out, like dogs on a hot day.

"Look," I said. "It's the Celeriac welcome committee."

Past the market was a little square with a fountain and two cafés facing each other from opposite sides of the street. The cafés were filled with men standing at the bar, and they were all shouting at the same time. I thought they were getting ready to have a big fight, but it turned out they were just discussing the weather and the latest soccer game.

In the middle of the square stood a man who was directing traffic. There was only one problem. There weren't any cars, since the street was closed for the open-air market. And if there had been cars, the drivers would not have known which way to go.

That's because the man, who was standing on one leg in the middle of the street, was moving his arms in all directions at once. First he pointed one way, then the other, like a weathervane on a windy day. Sometimes he pointed straight up to the sky!

"Hey, Roger-Roger!" someone shouted to him

from inside the café. "You forgot to change our calendar!"

Just like that, the man stopped his policeman imitation. He marched into the café with a very serious look on his face. Then he went behind the bar and pulled off a page from the calendar hanging on the wall. Everyone applauded, and he bowed.

Were they making fun of him? Or was this just normal life in our new village?

Roger-Roger marched out of the café and back into the street. He looked happy, as if he'd just accomplished a very important mission. Then he started directing traffic again.

I found out later that Roger-Roger got his name because he repeated everything twice, and that he'd been tearing off the pages of the café's calendar forever. That was his job in the village.

What a strange place this Celeriac was! I was beginning to wonder if there were any normal people here, doing normal things. I guess I'd just have to wait and see.

It turned out that we arrived just in time for the end-of-summer celebrations. That's the most important time of the year in a little village like Celeriac. All the villages have a celebration, and the goal is to do the craziest things possible, so that everyone has something to talk about all year, until the next celebration.

I should know. It happened right on our street.

One day, a truck pulled into the square by our house and started unloading metal barricades. You know, those metal fences with the ends that lock together.

By that time, my brother and I had met some of the other kids in the village. It turned out that there were young people in Celeriac after all. Not everybody spent their days on a stone bench by the cemetery, watching Linda the snoring speed bump sleeping in the sun.

The kids would meet on the square in front of the church, right near our house. It was the best spot in Celeriac, with giant plane trees that kept the place nice and shady. Most of the families in our part of the village came from North Africa. The kids' mothers all wore scarves on their heads. Every evening before dinner, the women would watch their kids play soccer. The goal was the front door of the church. If you shot the ball past the goalie, through the open door and into the church, you scored.

I was pretty surprised the first time I saw that happen. I know that Muslims don't go to church. They go to a mosque. But no one else in the village seemed to go to church either. And no one minded if we used its open door as a goal.

I became friends with two guys who played soccer, Rachid and Ahmed. When school began, we would be in the same class. I asked them about the barricades.

"That's for the bulls," Rachid said. "So they don't go where they're not supposed to."

"Bulls?" my brother asked. "On our street?"

He looked pretty worried, and for once I couldn't blame him.

"You'll see," Ahmed promised. "But don't worry, they'll knock on your door before they come in!"

"Sure they will," Rachid added. "With their horns!"

And they both started laughing.

The next weekend, a big banner went up above the square. It was tied from tree to tree.

Danger! Taureaux! it read. Danger! Bulls!

Then under it went another sign. *Welcome to the Celeriac Bull Festival! Have Fun!*

Get the picture? Danger! Have Fun! That says it all.

Early on the Saturday morning of the big bull festival, I was teaching my brother some soccer moves in the square. He wasn't very good, and I knew that if he was going to get along in Celeriac, he'd have to learn how to play.

I had just scored a church-door goal when two big heavy trucks pulled up. You couldn't see inside them because they were covered with a tarp, but you could sure smell what was in there.

We went over to get a closer look.

Just as my brother got close to the first truck, there was a tremendous crash inside it. The truck rocked from side to side, and for a moment I thought it would tip right over on top of him.

"Max! Run!" I yelled.

He took off across the square as if his pants were on fire.

But there was nothing to worry about. The truck was solid. There were just some bulls inside it, and they'd decided to play a very loud game of musical chairs.

Some men got out of the cab. French cowboys! They were wearing blue jeans, cowboy boots, black hats like the bad guys in the movies, and they had kerchiefs tied around their necks.

As the bulls stamped and snorted inside the

trucks, the men started setting up the barricades, fitting one piece into the other. They made good and sure that the fences were well connected to each other.

When they reached the pile of pieces by our little street, they started arguing.

Then they decided to move the fence back so our street would be part of the bull festival. Just great! Wild animals right on our doorstep.

"Cool," my brother said. He was acting brave again. "We'll have the best view in town."

"We'll have an even better view if the bulls decide to come and visit."

My brother looked worried again. It's so easy to tease him!

As we were having lunch, a pick-up truck came rolling through the village. It had a loudspeaker on its roof, and bullfight music was blaring out of it. The truck drove slowly along the narrow streets, inviting one and all to the exciting bull festival.

"The festival takes no responsibility for any accidents that might occur," the loudspeaker warned us after the final trumpet note faded away.

Unfortunately, our mother heard the warning. She set down her fork on her plate, next to the snails she was enjoying. Luckily, my brother and I were enjoying hot dogs. French hot dogs.

"I won't have either of you getting trampled by bulls. Whatever is going to happen out there, you can watch it from your bedroom window."

My brother and I groaned. That's my mother for you. She's always talking about experiencing new things, but when a real adventure comes along, she starts fussing and taking all the fun out of it.

By the time the end of the afternoon came around, the square was filled with people. From my bedroom window, we could see that everyone in the village was there, from the duck thief to the goat-cheese lady. People had come from all the nearby villages. It looked as though our town was the center of the world.

Everyone was squished against the barricades that were supposed to be bull-proof. Kids were hanging from the lamp posts and the street signs. Rachid and Ahmed had climbed a tree in the square, and they were watching from the lowest branch. Their big brothers were sitting on top of the phone booth on the bulls' side of the fence.

If we hung out far enough from the window, we could see the French cowboys riding past on beautiful white horses, followed by a large cloud of black flies. Everyone applauded.

I couldn't stand missing out on all the excitement. I nudged my brother with my elbow. We tiptoed past my mother's studio where she was busy drawing. She had to finish a picture for the end of the week, and when she draws, she's in a world of her own.

We ran down the stone stairway and out into the square. Rachid and Ahmed jumped out of their tree and came to say hello. We were all waiting for something dangerous to happen. And we didn't have to wait long.

The riders appeared again, keeping their horses close together. When they rode past us, I saw what they were escorting.

Bulls — real live bulls! They were enormous and powerful, and covered in black fur. Their horns were as sharp as razors, and as long as my arm. They snorted and bellowed as they ran down the street, and the riders had to be really good at their job to keep them from running wild. The riders were fearless, and their horses were, too.

Then Rachid and a bunch of other kids jumped over the fence.

"Come on, Ahmed!" Rachid called.

But Ahmed just rubbed his knee.

"My leg hurts," he told us.

Rachid and the other kids ran after the bulls. They grabbed their tails and pulled on them as hard as they could. Meanwhile, the riders urged the bulls forward. The bulls kept running, herded along by the horses. I think all the poor bulls wanted was to go back to their fields and eat some nice grass.

"Why are they teasing them?" I asked Ahmed.

"To make them mad," he explained, hanging on to the fence next to us. "Aren't there any bulls where you come from?"

"No."

"What do you do for fun?"

"Other things," I told him. "Plenty of other things."

But I couldn't think of anything as exciting as having real live bulls running wild on your street.

The next time the horses and bulls passed by, the riders pulled away, and the bulls were free to run wherever they wanted. That sure surprised the kids who were pulling their tails. Rachid came running back to the fence and vaulted over it. Let me tell you, he sure smelled like the rear end of a bull!

"Pee-yew!" my brother shouted, and he held his nose.

Rachid ran off to the fountain on the other side of the square to wash his hands. He came back a minute later.

"Okay, guys," he said to us, "this is the best part!"

The square was full of bulls, and they were spoiling for a fight. They were mad because kids had pulled their tails, and now they wanted to get even. They snorted and pawed the ground and dared anyone to come near.

"Do you think the fence is strong enough?" my brother asked with a little tremble in his voice.

"As long as you're on this side, they won't bother you," Ahmed told him. "They have much more appetizing targets."

Rachid jumped over the fence again, and he wasn't the only one. Half the village kids were out in the square, teasing the bulls and running like crazy in all directions.

They waved their arms and twirled their shirts and made funny faces at the bulls. The bulls didn't like that, and they would chase the kids, who would run like the wind for the nearest fence. They would jump back over it to safety, and the bull would stop, then go looking for another target.

Everyone was screaming and laughing, and the bullfight music was blaring away. What a racket!

I wanted to try, but on the other hand, I was scared. The bulls were enormous and they had these mean-looking little eyes.

I glanced over at Ahmed.

"Why aren't you out there?"

Ahmed rubbed his knee some more.

"My leg hurts, remember?"

I guess I wasn't the only one who was scared.

The bulls were galloping past at top speed, chasing the kids who were waving their T-shirts in their faces. Red T-shirts. You know those cartoons where someone waves a red flag at a bull? Well, it works in real life, too. Of course, any color will do. The bulls seem to like any moving target.

All of a sudden I realized that one of those moving targets was my father. He was running across the square with the rest of the kids. Let me tell you, he stuck out like a sore thumb.

"Mom's going to kill him!" my brother shouted.

"If a bull doesn't get him first."

Ahmed laughed. "That's your father?"

"I'm afraid so," I admitted. When would he stop embarrassing me?

"That's great!" Ahmed laughed. "Do you think my father would ever do anything like that? Never in a million years!"

I didn't know what to think. I was half ashamed and half proud. There was my father, chasing around the square with the kids from the village, teasing the bulls and running for his life.

There was only one problem. He wasn't very good at it.

And one particular bull seemed to know that.

Maybe this bull was smarter than the others.

Maybe he was just meaner. He kept dipping his horns and charging my father, and making sure he couldn't jump back over the fence to safety, where all the sane people were.

"We'd better do something," I said to my brother.

"Like what? Pull on the bull's tail so he'll leave Dad alone?"

"I don't know… There's got to be something. Something fast!"

The bull chased our father around a tree. He slipped on the pavement and for a second I thought the bull would trample him. I closed my eyes. When I opened them, my father was still on his feet, and the bull was still after him.

Then I saw the way out.

I climbed up on the fence.

"Dad! The phone booth!" I shouted as loud as I could.

He heard me. He turned and made a beeline for the phone booth. He got there just in time! The bulls' horns were practically grazing his back pocket.

Everyone was pointing and shouting.

"Olé! Bravo! *Vive le Canadien!*"

"That's a great idea," Ahmed told me. "He can phone the firemen to come and save him."

"What if he doesn't have any change?" Max asked.

My brother never stops worrying.

The bull took a few steps back. He snorted and pawed the ground and made scary bull noises. He wanted to attack, but he wasn't too sure how to go about it. There probably weren't too many phone booths in the field where he lived.

Meanwhile, Rachid's and Ahmed's older brothers were sitting on top of the phone booth, smoking cigarettes and looking very casual. They started yelling things at the bull.

"The phone is busy, *monsieur le taureau*," they said, holding out their cellphones. "Want to use ours? As long as it's not long distance."

The bull turned his head to one side, as if he really were trying to understand. He looked at the shiny cellphone. Then he turned toward the phone booth, lowered his head, snorted and started pawing the ground.

My father was caught in a trap. I had to do something!

That's when I scrambled over the fence and ran toward the bull. I slapped him on his backside as hard as I could. The bull turned around and roared.

I didn't stick around to see if he was chasing me. I sprinted for the fence, then squeezed underneath.

That was when my father made his escape.

With the bull looking the other way, he rushed out of the phone booth and ran to the fence. He put both hands on the railing and vaulted right over the top.

I never knew he could do something like that. I guess fear gives you new talents!

My father was completely out of breath. He wiped his red face with his torn shirtsleeve.

"Thanks, Charlie," he panted. "That was a good idea."

"He saved your life!" my brother piped up.

"Do me a favor, okay, guys? Don't tell your mother."

But trying to keep a secret in a village like ours was impossible. By the end of the day, the story had been repeated dozens of times. It was just too good not to tell. Everyone appreciated my father because he'd given them something to laugh about, at least until next year.

And I became a hero because I'd helped save him.

FOUR

We are almost washed away by a flood

The next week, it started to rain. It rained every day and every night, non-stop. People think that the sun always shines in southern France. But I'd never seen rain like that in my whole life.

Everyone in the village was very worried about the grape harvest. If it rains too much on the grapes before it's time to pick them, the wine won't be as good. Don't ask me why. That's just the way it is.

One morning at six-thirty, a strange sound woke me up. I opened my eyes and went to the window. A helicopter was hovering in the rainy sky above our village. The helicopter was carrying a pair of wild-eyed, rust-colored horses on a swing-ing platform.

The sound woke my brother up, too.

"What's going on?"

"Two horses are flying over our house," I told him.

"No way!" he said.

He rushed over to the window. By then the horses had disappeared over the neighbors' roof, but we could still hear them neighing. And it was raining cats and dogs.

We went downstairs. I didn't see my father. He must have been sleeping. A helicopter wouldn't wake him up unless it landed on his bed. My mother was in the kitchen, wearing a raincoat and huge rubber boots. She was completely soaked. There was a puddle of water on the floor.

"Did you see the flying horses?" my brother asked.

"Yes," she said. "They're being evacuated because of the Vidourle. The river has overflowed, and it's flooded most of the village. We're on high ground, so we're all right – so far, anyway."

"Cool!" Max shouted.

Then he did a little rain-dance, as if we needed it.

"Put your boots on," she said. "Let's go out and see what's happening."

We all stepped outside and into the rain. First we crossed the square. Water was bubbling up around the trees, as if they were drinking fountains.

We met Rachid. He was watching our soccer field disappear under the water.

"Want to play?" I asked him.

"Sure. Submarine soccer. But we'd need snorkel masks."

We moved down the street toward the Vidourle. But halfway there, we had to stop. The pavement was covered in muddy brown water. All kinds of things were floating in the flooded street. Tree branches and logs, wine bottles, of course. A metal frame from a bed, the hood of a car, a table from a sidewalk café — you name it.

Then I saw my father in the middle of the flooded street, with the water up past his knees. He wasn't sleeping after all.

On both sides of the street, people were leaning out of their second-floor windows. They were in a complete panic.

"*On va se noyer!*" a woman was shouting. "We're going to drown!"

But she couldn't have been too scared, since she'd opened her umbrella first so she wouldn't get soaked.

I marched into the water. I wasn't sure what I was going to do, but I wanted to be part of the

action. Before long, the water was pouring over the top of my boots. I had my own private flood in my shoes.

"Stay where you are!" my mother called to the woman. "The water will never reach the second floor."

"I have to save my things downstairs before the water comes into the house," she cried.

I looked at the front door. It was too late. The muddy brown flood had already pushed open the door and invited itself in. I tried to close the door, but there's nothing stronger than fast-flowing water.

Then I saw the woman with the umbrella coming down the stairs inside her house. She gasped when she saw the water in the living room. I couldn't blame her. In the middle of the room, her very unhappy cat was sitting on top of a floating armchair, meowing its head off.

"*Mon petit minou,*" the woman cried. "I'll save you."

I saw the whole scene as if it were in slow motion, just like in the movies. The woman coming down the stairs with her dripping umbrella. The cat meowing on top of the chair that was about to capsize. The lamp on the floor with its lightbulb burning. And the rising water about to reach the wall outlet.

Water and electricity don't mix. Everyone learns that in science class.

"Stop!" I shouted to the woman. "*Arrêtez!* It's too dangerous! You could get electrocuted!"

She stopped and looked at me. I could tell she didn't believe me. After all, I was just a kid.

My mother came running up behind me.

"He's right, Madame Dentmouillée," she called to the woman. "If the water touches the lamp... Go back upstairs. We'll call the fire department."

The woman retreated back up the stairway, very slowly, keeping an eye on the water as if it were a sea monster.

"But... but, *mon minou*," she whispered. "He'll drown!"

"Just stay where you are," I told the cat. "You'll be okay, too."

But the poor cat was desperate. You know how cats hate water! He took a flying leap from the top of the armchair and landed on the fourth step of the stairway, which was still dry. Madame Dentmouillée picked him up and nearly hugged him to death.

Out in the street, my mother patted me on the shoulder.

"You saved her life, you know. It doesn't matter if she didn't believe you. *You* know, and that's what counts."

I took off my boots and turned them upside down. Along with the dirty-brown water came a handful of tiny silver minnows no bigger than my little finger.

We moved down the street barefoot, looking for more people to save. We came upon a group of people standing around the front door of someone's house. I looked inside, since everyone else was.

I couldn't believe it. Water was shooting up through the stone floor of the kitchen. Underground springs were coming to the surface. The ground under our village must have had more holes in it than a Swiss cheese!

Meanwhile, the people were sweeping the water out of the house and into the street with brooms and shovels and dustpans. Just as quickly, the kitchen filled up with water again.

"I don't get it," my brother said. "Where's all the water coming from? It's hardly even raining any more."

"The problem is in the mountains," my mother explained. "There were big storms up there last night. That's where all this water is coming from."

Marco, the man who ran the grocery store down the street, had another idea.

"It's not the mountains' fault. I'll tell you whose fault it is! That guy Arthur who runs the dam upriver. He fell asleep at the switch and let all the water go by!"

"They spend millions building the dam to keep us from getting flooded. Then they hire some donkey to run it, and he falls asleep," said our neighbor, Monsieur Mendes.

"Arthur likes his wine too much. That's the problem," Marco concluded.

Everybody started arguing about whose fault it was, and complaining about the man who had fallen asleep at the switch. I sure wouldn't want to be him!

Meanwhile, my brother slipped into the flooded house to look at the underground springs that had taken over the kitchen. Sure enough, as he was bending over and trying to see exactly where the water was coming from, he fell head first, right into it.

Splash!

For a very long couple of seconds, he didn't get up.

"That's where the old well is!" Marco shouted.

And he pulled my brother out of the water.

Poor Max. He'd fallen right into the spot where a well had been, in the center of the kitchen. Not only was he soaked, but his knee was bleeding badly. And he was trying really hard not to cry.

"We'd better get you cleaned up," my mother

said to him. "I don't like the way that cut looks, not with all this dirty water."

Marco looked at his watch.

"You're in luck, Madame," he told my mother. "Dr. Rosalie comes by every day at this time to look after the people in the old folks' home."

We stepped outside again. My mother was holding my soaked brother. Just then, a rowboat with two men in it sailed past us. They had a dog with them that was barking its head off. I guess animals don't like floods.

"How is a doctor going to get here, with all this water?" my mother asked.

"You don't know Dr. Rosalie. She never misses an appointment. Rain or shine."

Sure enough, Marco was right. A few minutes later, a Jeep came driving very slowly down the flooded street. Brown water was lapping around the bottom of its doors.

Marco waved his arms and the Jeep stopped, pushing waves of water ahead of it. A woman in a white coat was sitting at the wheel.

"Dr. Rosalie!" Marco shouted. "We have a little emergency for you."

The woman stepped out. I'd never seen a doctor like her. She was wearing a white coat and high rubber boots past her knees — the kind fishermen wear.

She didn't waste any time. She asked my brother what his name was, and if he was scared. Then she set him on the hood of the Jeep. She put her doctor's bag next to him and got to work.

"When a doctor tells you that it's not going to hurt, do you believe it?" she asked Max.

"No." He shook his head.

"Smart boy!" she said.

She cleaned his cut and gave him a tetanus shot. That must have hurt! She bandaged up his knee. Then Dr. Rosalie hopped back in her Jeep and splashed down the street.

"We didn't even pay her," my mother said.

Marco laughed. "Don't worry! You'll see her again. This is a small town."

The rowboat came past again. This time, the men were paddling as fast as they could the other way.

"The Vidourle's leaving," one of the men in the rowboat called out over the barking dog. "The water's going down!"

I looked down the street. Sure enough, the water was retreating fast, as if someone had pulled the plug in a bathtub.

In fact, the water went down so fast that a small school of silvery fish were stranded on the street. They flopped around on the pavement, wondering where their water had disappeared to.

My brother took a few steps, trying out his new limp. He looked down at his bandage. He was very proud of it.

At the end of the street, we met up with Madame Mendes. She was talking with my mother.

"All this rain makes me think of poor old Madame Chaudeoreille," she said in a sad voice.

In case you didn't know, *Chaudeoreille* means "hot ear." Can you imagine having that for a name?

"Who is she?" my mother asked.

"That poor old lady who drowned in your house."

"Who drowned?" my little brother butted in.

"*La pauvre dame*," our neighbor said. "Poor lady."

But she had this happy look in her eyes. She must have been waiting forever for a morning just like this one to tell us the story.

"Her son and daughter-in-law lived upstairs, where you do. But she, you understand, she was in a wheelchair. One night the waters rose, just like this, except much worse. It was night, she couldn't move, the Vidourle came into the house, her son was upstairs sleeping with his new bride… You can imagine the rest."

"Do you think her ghost still lives in our house?" my brother asked.

"A ghost?" Madame Mendes said. "I couldn't say..."

"When did all this happen?" my mother asked.

"Oh, I was just a girl at the time... That would be nearly seventy years ago, maybe more."

"If there was a ghost, we'd know about it by now," my little brother decided. He looked relieved.

"Poor old lady," our neighbor was saying. "When I think of her helpless in her chair, and the waters rising, and her son sleeping upstairs..."

I thought she was going to cry. But right in the middle of her sad story, she reached down and snatched a couple of fish off the pavement. She slipped them into a plastic bag that she just happened to have in her purse. They looked suspiciously like the little fish Madame Mendes and her husband liked to eat.

Just then my father came walking up.

"Well, no one drowned and no one got electrocuted. It's time for breakfast, kids," he said. "I'm starving."

"We're not having fish, are we?" I asked.

"Since when do we eat fish for breakfast?"

My mother and I tried to keep from laughing, but it was too late.

As we went into our house, I heard a dog barking and two men complaining in loud voices. I went to the end of our little street to see what was going on. The two men were lugging the heavy rowboat in their arms. And in it, as unhappy as ever, their dog was barking up a storm.

The Great Flood was over.

FIVE

Reading, writing and… fighting!

$\mathcal{T}$ wo days after the Great Flood, school started. I was pretty nervous about starting a new school. I had met some of the kids who lived in the village, but this was a big school attended by students from all over the countryside. I would be the only foreigner. My brother wouldn't be there, since he would be going to the little grade school.

I would be the new kid, *le Canadien*, the one with the funny accent and the weird parents who didn't seem to work for a living. All the other kids had parents who grew grapes or built houses or took care of animals. Writing and drawing all day long was not considered real work in this part of the world.

That's why the school year started slowly in Celeriac. Half the kids were busy harvesting grapes in the vineyards. They did it to help their families and neighbors, and of course they made a little money, too. That came in handy, because there weren't too many ways for kids to make money in the village. No paper routes or leaf-raking or snow-shoveling like in Montreal.

Little by little, kids started showing up at school with sun-burned faces and purple hands. Some of them even had purple hair, and it wasn't because they were punk rockers. At the end of the harvest, they "washed" each other all over with grapes. That was their way of celebrating the end of the job.

School turned out to be very different in Celeriac. On the first morning, the kids showed up and shook hands with each other. They introduced themselves, first name and last, very politely, like little businessmen.

But when lunchtime came around, they got together to fight in the schoolyard. They fought like animals! There were no rules. And what's more, they were allowed to fight. In my school back home, you could get expelled for it. Here, the teachers even supervised the fights!

That was one of the not-very-civilized things about France, which was supposed to be such a civilized place.

I never understood why the kids fought. Everything seemed to follow a kind of secret code that I didn't get. Maybe they fought because they'd fought the year before, or because their fathers had fought, or their grandfathers before them.

I was lucky, because I had a friend named Daniel, the son of Didier the science teacher, who played on the same soccer team as my father. If someone tried to push me around, Daniel would step in and stop it.

"Not him, he's a guest," he would tell the other kid. "You can't fight a foreigner."

And just like that, the kid would disappear, like magic.

Daniel knew more about the world than the rest of the kids in the village. His family had traveled. He had even gone dog-sledding with his parents in northern Canada, something I'd never done. Daniel wanted to be an environmentalist, and he said that there was more environment in Canada.

I thought being a foreigner would be a problem, but it actually turned out to be an advantage, especially with the girls.

In Montreal, girls my age wouldn't talk to boys.

But in Celeriac, they weren't shy at all. Maybe it was because I had a different accent, or maybe it was because I had been to places other kids had never seen, but suddenly I was popular with girls. They would even follow me home in the afternoon and wait for me in front of my house in the morning.

After our first English class, I became even more popular. The English teacher discovered that I spoke English better than she did. She got very embarrassed and upset, and the rest of the kids loved that.

The teacher had another problem, but it really wasn't her fault. Her name was Madame Grondin. A *grondin* is an extremely ugly pink fish with big scales and a gigantic mouth and long whiskers. You can see one in the market if you don't look away in time.

Poor Madame Grondin! Not only did she have a name that made everyone laugh, but her English was really bad. In fact, it was terrible.

She must have learned her English out of a book, and she'd probably never heard the language spoken by real people. I didn't mean to correct her, but the words slipped out of my mouth before I could stop them.

"Now, children," she began, "you will use your crayons to write your exercises."

"A crayon is for coloring in coloring books," I told her. "You want to say pencil."

She looked totally outraged.

"Perhaps *monsieur* would like to learn the class himself?" she suggested.

"No, but I could *teach* it," I corrected her.

I realized I'd gone too far when her eyes started bulging out.

"*Pardon, Madame,*" I said.

But by then, everyone — especially the girls — was laughing and applauding.

After that, every afternoon there would be a knock on our door. My mother stood behind me, smiling, as I opened the door to find a group of girls who wanted help with their English homework. It was embarrassing, the way she was so delighted that I had visitors. But luckily she didn't hang around too long. Not like Max, who stuck to me like glue. After they finished their homework, the girls would ask me about the English songs they listened to. What did the words mean? It must be strange to listen to music and not understand the words.

My brother wouldn't stop teasing me about the girls. I never fought at school, but I made up for it by fighting with him at home.

I also helped Rachid and Ahmed and some of

the other soccer players. After our homework was done, they would lend me a pole and we would go fishing in the river that had calmed down after the flood. The little fish we caught tasted like mud, and you'd have to be dying of hunger to eat one. But it was lots of fun. I never got to go fishing in Montreal.

Little by little, I began to feel at home. My mother started to give free drawing lessons to the kids on Wednesday mornings, when there was no school and their parents were working. My father joined the village soccer team, even though he had never played soccer in his life.

One day when I was hanging out on the square,

kicking the ball back and forth with Rachid, one
of the red-faced men who spent his days in the café
shouted out to me, "Hey, kid, you play better than
your father! You should give him some lessons."

Well, at least my father was trying!

One afternoon, as I was coming back from
school with my friends, I could hear my father's
typewriter chattering away through the open window.

"I guess your father doesn't have a job," Ahmed said. "Mine doesn't either."

"My father's a writer," I told him. "He works all the time, even on vacations."

"That's not a real job," Rachid said. "He doesn't have a schedule or a boss or anything."

"People wonder how your family gets along with neither of your parents working," Ahmed added. "At least my mom works."

"So does mine. She writes stories and draws pictures."

Ahmed, Rachid and my new friend Florian, Dr. Rosalie's son, looked at each other and shrugged. They weren't convinced.

"Then how come your mother rides around on her bike in the mountains every afternoon? My mother would never do that," Florian laughed.

What could I say? My parents were different. Anyway, I was used to having them embarrass me.

One of the ways you could fit in was to participate in the local cultural activities. Nearly all of them had to do with food.

Sometimes we went to the sea coast, an hour away by car. But instead of lying on the beach or flying kites, we had to participate in clam-digging expeditions. The clams were no bigger than your thumbnail, and you caught them by running a

rake through the sand, which had a mesh bag attached to it.

Other times we went into the mountains, where chestnut trees grew. We filled sacks full of chestnuts for roasting.

The only thing we didn't participate in was the boar hunt. A boar is a kind of wild pig that likes to eat grapes. Actually, they look like pigs with tusks, and they walk on their tiptoes, as if they were wearing high-heeled shoes. To hunt them, you had to have a licence. Luckily, we didn't have one.

When it rained, we went snail-hunting, because snails just love rain. I followed my parents through the rocky vineyards as they and their village friends pinched the snails off the wilted leaves of the grapevines and dumped them into buckets.

Snail-hunting was easy, but things got more complicated when Madame Mendes showed up after the hunt with a wire mesh cage and set it up in our kitchen.

"*Il faut les faire baver*," she cackled. "You have to make them drool."

"Snail-drool?" said Max. "Disgusting!"

He immediately tried to imitate a drooling snail. He was right. It was disgusting!

Meanwhile, Madame Mendes dumped several pailfuls of snails into the cage.

That was my introduction to Celeriac snail technology. After you caught the snails, which wasn't hard because they aren't too fast, you had to help them get rid of whatever was in their little snail stomachs before you could eat them. They had to drool, as Madame Mendes put it.

While they were busy drooling, we were supposed to feed them herbs so that they would taste good when their big day came, which was in a couple of weeks. That was my brother's job. But every time he gave them their branches of rosemary and thyme, a few of them would "accidentally" escape.

He would run around the kitchen as if his pants were on fire.

"Get back here!" he called. "I'll catch you yet!"

What a clown!

Crunch!

One of us would dash into the kitchen to see what was going on and step on a snail. That usually happened just before dinner. Nothing like squished snail on a stone floor to take away your appetite!

One Friday afternoon in the late autumn, a sunny day after several days of rain, Marco stopped me as I was walking past his grocery store.

"*Mon garçon*," he began, "do you know what it smells like?"

And he sniffed the air and smiled.

That's the way people were in Celeriac. They always asked questions you couldn't answer.

I sniffed the air, too. It smelled like air to me.

"No," I admitted.

"It smells like mushrooms," he said happily. "Definitely, it smells like mushrooms."

"I see."

"How would you like to go mushroom-hunting tomorrow?"

"All right," I said. "But don't you have to work in your store?"

He waved his hands in the air. "The store can take a day off, too. Tell your parents they're invited. We'll leave at eight. I want to get to the best spots before anyone else does."

Marco had a little grocery store, but selling food wasn't his main interest in life. Whenever

there was a postcard show, or a meeting of the his-
torical society, or if the day was perfect for walking
in the mountains, or if there was the smell of
mushrooms in the air, he would simply close his
shop and disappear for the day.

Still, a lot of people depended on him.
Sometimes they would show up at the counter –
he didn't have a cash register, and he added up the
totals by hand – with their basket full of food, and
admit shyly that they didn't quite have enough
money to pay.

"Don't worry," he would tell them. "I'll put it
on your bill."

Half the time, he never asked his customers for
money if he knew they couldn't pay. Once I saw
Rachid's mother march into the store and happily
put a small mountain of bills on the counter.

"For the past couple of months," she told him.
"We're even now."

The mountains and the forests were his favorite
places to be, and he knew their secrets. Sometimes
he would drive down from the mountains above
our village and start unloading goat cheeses from a
box full of straw that he kept in the back of his old
truck. He'd point to the runny cheeses that smelled
like the boys' locker room at school.

"I had to get out for some fresh air on my way
down here. I couldn't stay in my truck another

minute. Those cheeses sure aren't embarrassed to be who they are!"

A little like Marco himself.

In the end, I understood what he meant about the air smelling like mushrooms. After an hour's drive in the back of his beat-up delivery truck, squished in with Tempo, his very furry dog, and being rocked this way and that, we got out at the edge of an oak forest.

After that, we hiked for another hour on a stone path that had been used by people and their donkeys for centuries – or at least that's what Marco told us. Everything in France is so old!

We finally reached his secret spot. It was in a wide clearing in the middle of the woods, surrounded by giant trees. Just the way snails like rain, mushrooms like oak trees.

Suddenly the rays of the sun filled the clearing, and I could smell a rich, woodsy, earth smell.

"*Boletus edulis!*" Marco exclaimed.

That's the Latin name for the mushrooms we were hunting. Big fat ones, as wide as the palm of my hand. Having Marco as a guide was very useful, because he showed us which mushrooms tasted good and which ones would kill you dead before dessert. Pretty important information, don't you think?

Though Marco would never tell anyone else

about his secret mushroom-hunting spots, he was willing to share them with us. That's because we were foreigners, he said. He wanted us to see all the best things in his part of the country. He also knew that we were here only for the year, so his secret spots were safe with us.

Sometimes, being a foreigner can be a real advantage.

Six

Christmas time in our village

One morning, I was awoken by the screechy voice of Madame Mendes talking to her dog.

"No, no, no," she scolded Linda. "You can't go out. You'll freeze your little paws in the snow."

Snow? I thought to myself. How can that be?

I rushed to the window and looked out. Sure enough, there was snow, but barely enough to cover the ground. I went to the back window and looked out there, too. Everything was white, even the little palm tree in our yard.

Rachid came running down our narrow street.

When he reached the front door of our house, he tripped and slid head-first on the snow that covered the paving stones. It would have been a perfect slide if he'd been playing baseball, which of course he wasn't.

"Hey, Charlie!" he shouted from below. "There's no school today. Classes are canceled!"

"How come?" I called down.

"What do you mean, how come?"

He got up and brushed the snow off his jacket. Then he stared up at me as if I were blind.

"Look! Can't you see?" He waved his hands in the air like a windmill. "It's because of the snowstorm."

Snowstorm? I thought. This wouldn't even be a blip on the snow radar screen back home. There were no cars buried up to their roofs in snow, and no drifts that you had to shovel your way through just to get out of the house.

But I didn't say anything. Rachid was so excited that I didn't want to disappoint him.

I went downstairs, grabbed my jacket and went outside. It was the kind of snow that was mostly made of water. If you squeezed it real hard in your hand, there wouldn't be much left. But apparently, this was a blizzard for Celeriac.

Ahmed came running up, too, but he managed to stay on his two feet.

"I've never seen snow," he said, "except on TV."

Madame Mendes opened her front door a crack.

"Be careful, boys," she warned us, "or you'll get lost in the storm!"

Before we could answer, she slammed her door tight, then locked it.

My brother stepped out, pulling on his jacket.

"Have you ever seen snow before?" Ahmed asked him.

"Maybe once or twice," Max told him.

"Come on," Rachid teased Ahmed. "He's from Canada, remember?"

"Sure," I said, "we live in igloos. But only during the winter."

Ahmed didn't know whether to believe me or not.

We crossed the square where we played soccer. Just then, a big clump of snow fell right on Ahmed's head, slid past the collar of his jacket and ran down his back. He jumped.

"Who did that?" he asked, looking around.

"The trees," my brother laughed.

That gave me an idea.

"Let me show you what we do when it snows," I told Rachid and Ahmed.

I bent down and made a snowball. I took aim, fired. Bull's eye! I hit Max right in the shoulder,

but not too hard. He fired back, but I dodged his snowball, and it hit the tree behind me.

"Cool!" Rachid yelled.

Let me tell you, it didn't take him and Ahmed long to learn how to have a real snowball fight.

We decided to go exploring. We headed toward the main square where the fountain and the cafés were.

Just then, old Monsieur Vilain came careening past us on his bicycle, down the slippery street. He

was headed down the slope that runs toward the
Vidourle, and fast.

"Help!" he called. "I can't stop! My brakes…"

We lost sight of him at the edge of the river,
where benches stand along the side of a low wall.

"He fell into the river," my brother said. "He's
going to drown!"

We started running down the street, following
Monsieur Vilain's wobbly tire tracks. My brother's
always exaggerating. But we decided to go and see
anyway.

At first, because of the wall, we couldn't see anything. But we sure could hear a lot! The ducks were all quacking angrily. They hated to be disturbed, especially by an old guy on a bike who had ridden right into them. And we could hear him, too.

"Confounded snow!" he muttered. "The brakes don't work at all… Never saw anything like it! The weather's gone crazy, that's for sure."

We peered over the edge of the wall. Luckily, it wasn't far down. There was Monsieur Vilain brushing himself off as the ducks crowded around him, quacking in outrage and nipping at his pants.

"Are you all right?" I asked him.

He looked up at me.

"You're the Canadian kid, aren't you? This must be your fault. Did you send us all this snow?"

"Really, it's not very much," I told him. "Can I help?"

He lifted his bicycle and we grabbed it from above. Then we all pulled and tugged until we had it back on the street. He climbed up the set of steps in the wall and took his bike from us without even saying thank you. I guess he really did blame us for the snow.

We walked back through the town. The cars were skidding and sliding every which way. People sure didn't know how to drive in winter here! They could have used Roger-Roger to help them out, but he was too afraid of the snow. I saw him standing in the doorway of the café. He was wearing a hat made out of a soggy newspaper, and he was staring nervously at the fat flakes that were falling from the sky.

In the distance, we started hearing sirens. Lots of them. We followed the sound and came to the edge of Celeriac, where the town's only traffic light stood. The snow must have done something to it, because the light was green for everyone. And there were two cars and a truck in the ditch.

I recognized the truck. It belonged to Marco. He had climbed through the back door, and now he was trying to get his dog Tempo out, but Tempo was in too much of a panic to listen. He was barking up a storm.

Then I saw Didier, Daniel's father, trying to push one of the cars out of the ditch all by himself. Meanwhile, the drivers were standing by the side of the road, shouting and waving their hands in the air. At least no one was badly hurt. The police were trying to get everyone to calm down, but since they were shouting and waving their hands in the air, too, they weren't very much help.

In the middle of the crowd, I saw Dr. Rosalie checking people's arms and legs to make sure no one had any broken bones.

She waved to us.

"Enjoying the storm?" she called out.

"It's just a little snow," I answered.

"Maybe for you."

Then she went back to work. She was having a hard time examining the drivers, because they didn't want to stop arguing about whose fault the accident was.

"Let's go by the school," I suggested. "And organize a snowball fight like in *The Dog Who Stopped the War*."

"Nobody will be there," Ahmed said. "The

schoolbuses didn't come in because of the snow-storm."

But no one had any better ideas, so we trudged through the snow, which barely came up to the edge of my sneakers, in the direction of school. Maybe there would be a few kids from the village.

As we walked along, the clouds started to lift and the sun shone through.

"If we're going to have a snowball fight, we'd better hurry up," I said.

And sure enough, by noon there wasn't a single snowflake left. The Great Celeriac Blizzard was over.

Christmas was different in Celeriac. First of all, there were no decorations. No colored lights, and not a single plastic Santa Claus. It wasn't like in our neighborhood back home, where there were contests to see who could put up the brightest lights, and where the Christmas decorations went up right after Halloween.

No wonder! No one celebrated Halloween here either.

The square where we played soccer had a church, but all year long it seemed as if no one ever went inside except for us kids, when one of us scored a goal through the open front door. But a few days before Christmas, people seemed to wake up and remember that the church was there. Women started going in and out with brooms and dustpans and buckets. After they were finished, men came in with boards and bales of hay. We heard hammering from inside.

Now that the Great Blizzard was over, the temperature had warmed up again, and my brother and I and Rachid and Ahmed were watching the preparations from outside.

"They're fixing it up for Midnight Mass," I told them.

"I've never been in a church," Ahmed said. "Not even to get the ball."

"I always have to chase down the ball," Rachid teased him, "even if he scores the goal. It's not fair."

"Just go in," Max told Ahmed.

"My father doesn't want me to."

"Why not?" I asked him.

"He just doesn't," said Ahmed. Then he looked away.

I knew Rachid and Ahmed were Muslims, which meant they didn't go to church. They went to a mosque, but I didn't even know if there was one in Celeriac. They never talked about it.

Our family liked celebrations. If there was a holiday to celebrate, we were always ready. My mother is Catholic and my father is Jewish, so I'm a little of both. My grandmother says that I have my father's eyes and my mother's nose. It's sort of the same thing. Anyway, we end up with two sets of holidays, which is fine with me.

That night, we got ready for Midnight Mass. We were going to be part of it. Our Midnight Mass, it turned out, didn't actually start at midnight. There was only one priest for all the little towns around ours, so he was very busy on Christmas Eve. Père Plomteux had to say Mass in one town after another, so he couldn't stay in any church for very long.

Ours was scheduled to start at ten o'clock. First, the organ music started. The organ was very old and out of tune. The organist, Monsieur Poire, had hair sprouting out of his ears and nose and big, bushy eyebrows. Actually, he looked like Santa Claus, but without a beard. As the kids paraded past him, he shouted orders at them. Monsieur Poire shouted because he was deaf. He didn't hear himself, but we sure did!

A lot of the kids from the village played in the Nativity scene. Pipo, the goalie on our team, played Joseph. He's always getting red cards during our games for arguing too much. Madame Soulier's daughter carried the baby Jesus. She was wearing a long dress, which she tripped over, and nearly fell. Everybody in the church gasped. At least Pipo could have caught the baby if she'd dropped him, since he's a pretty good goalie. Other kids from school wore gold paper crowns. They were the Three Wise Men.

Even Max and I got to play a part. Max was a sheep and I was a camel. We didn't have to speak, or even dress up, and that was just as well, because I wouldn't have wanted to wear a camel costume. All we had to do was carry our animals, that were actually little figurines, and place them in the manger. That wasn't too hard. Still, my mother looked on proudly as we walked past her.

Putting up with the organ music was a lot harder. I wouldn't have called it music at all. It sounded as though Monsieur Poire was playing with his elbows and his knees. No one could make him stop, since he couldn't hear everyone complaining.

Finally, Père Plomteux arrived. He looked as if he was in a big hurry. He went over to the organist and tapped him hard on the shoulder. The church went silent. Max and I walked up to the manger and held up our animals, and the other kids from the village started saying their lines.

But before Joseph and Mary could finish saying what they were supposed to, the organist started torturing his instrument again. The priest was angry because everything was taking too much time. He tapped the organist on the shoulder, twice as hard. The kids started laughing, though

Max and I didn't dare. We were afraid of being impolite, though I think we were the only ones who worried about that. Even the adults were laughing at the organist.

Finally the Mass was over. Père Plomteux practically ran out the door, his robes flying, on his way to the next village. Meanwhile, Monsieur Poire chased everyone out by playing as loudly and as badly as he could.

Outside, I spotted Rachid and Ahmed sitting on a bench, waiting for us. They looked a little lonely.

"How was it?" Rachid asked me.

"Noisy," I told him, "and pretty funny."

"Funny?" said Ahmed. "They do funny things in a church?"

I told him about the organist.

"And I got to be a sheep," Max piped up.

"I'm not surprised," Rachid teased him. "With that curly hair of yours, you look like a sheep."

Max was mad. "Yeah, well, Charlie was a camel!"

My brother made a camel face and bobbed his head up and down. Rachid and Ahmed nearly fell off the bench laughing.

"What do you guys do in a mosque?" I asked them.

Rachid shrugged. "We pray. We listen to the imam."

"But it's not funny," Ahmed added. "Not like in a church."

Just then, my mother came to get us.

"Let's go. Your father is making dinner and it's probably waiting."

We waved goodnight to our friends and headed home. My mother was right. Dinner was on the table. A roast pheasant stuffed with chestnuts that we'd gathered ourselves in the forest. It was really good, especially since I was so hungry. No wonder! It was nearly eleven o'clock at night.

But we had one more holiday to celebrate. My father had made a menorah out of the foot of a grape vine, which looks a lot like a tree trunk, only thinner. In each of the knots of the trunk, he placed a candle. There were eight of them, because it was the eighth night of Channukah, the last one, that just happened to fall on Christmas Eve.

Then our parents told us what our Christmas present was. And you won't believe it…

SEVEN
The never-ending journey

*Y*ou guessed it. Our Christmas present was another trip!

And there sure was lots of time to travel, with all the vacations we had.

"The schools are closed half the time," my mother complained. "There's this holiday, and that vacation. I wonder if you'll learn anything at all this year."

I thought we were working hard enough. There was homework nearly every night. If you ask me, they made us work double time to make up for all the vacations.

My father announced, "You know, kids, we haven't been anywhere for a while."

"What do you mean?" I asked him. "We're *here*. And we only just got here."

I was starting to enjoy life in our village, and I was in no hurry to pull up stakes again.

"You know what I mean," he said. "Some place new and different."

"Something new happens here all the time," I told him.

"Sure," my brother chimed in. "Yesterday I found a snail under the living-room sofa."

As usual, my parents didn't listen to me. They hadn't listened when they'd planned this trip. And now, when I was finally feeling comfortable here, and actually liking it a little, I had to leave again.

So off we went. At first things weren't as bad as I thought they'd be. In Europe the countries are really close together. You can drive for a couple of hours, and the language, the food, the buildings and the landscape change completely. Unfortunately, everything went a little more slowly in our car. It gasped going uphill, and rattled going down. Even the donkeys went faster than us as we headed toward our destination. Spain, and the city of Barcelona.

Barcelona is a pretty weird-looking place. That's because of this architect named Antoni Gaudí. The strange buildings he designed are all over the city. Some of them are crooked, and others are wavy. Some have all sorts of colorful columns and ceramic chimneys on the roofs, which is odd, since you can't see the roof from the street.

"Why is everything so crooked here?" asked my brother. "Was there an earthquake or something?"

"This Gaudí guy built his buildings before rulers were invented," I told him.

And he actually believed me!

We went to Güell Park that sits on a hill above the city. Gaudí designed the park, so of course it was full of curly-cue ceramic sculptures and railings that squirmed and slithered like snakes. There wasn't a straight line in the whole place.

My brother sat down on a bench. Not only did it have two humps like a camel, it was covered with tiny square tiles, all of them different colors, that fit together like a jigsaw puzzle.

"I don't like Gaudí's stuff," he said.

"Why not?" my mother asked.

"It makes me dizzy. And it looks like somebody's guts."

My brother had a point. But I think Gaudí was brave to invent buildings that were so different from everything else. People must have laughed at him at the time.

After the park, we went to see his famous church, La Sagrada Familia. Unfortunately, Señor

Gaudí never got around to completing it. And now people come from all over the world to see this half-built building and marvel over it, even though it's still unfinished. I don't get it. Imagine if I didn't finish my homework. Nobody would marvel over that!

Even though Barcelona is in Spain, people don't speak Spanish there. They speak Catalán, a language that looks a little like Spanish, but doesn't sound anything like it. They've taken most of the vowels out of Spanish and replaced them with consonants.

Catalán would be a great language for Scrabble. That's because of all the X's. As in *xocolata*. (Hint: you pronounce the "x" as if it were a "sh.") You could tally up some really big scores with words like that, though you'd have to have more X's in your game.

After we had our fill of Gaudí, we went to the Dali Museum just outside Barcelona. Salvador Dali is an artist who's famous for painting melting watches and some really weird landscapes. According to my mother, all artists have their own vision of the world, which changes the way we see things.

If that's true, my mom's vision of the world must be pretty weird, too. In some of her drawings, cats can fly and rabbits ride bicycles. I've never seen that happen, any more than I've seen melting watches.

But I'm keeping my eyes open.

The Dali museum was completely crazy inside and out. It looked like a huge pink castle with croissants growing out of the walls and gigantic eggs perched along the edge of the roof. I imagined one of those eggs falling and landing on us. The headlines would read, "Canadian Family Squished by Giant Egg."

That sure would change my vision of the world!

After Barcelona, my parents decided to go to Andalucia, in the very south of Spain. I was ready to go back to Celeriac. I missed my friends already. Most of all, I was tired of traveling in our beat-up sardine can of a car.

"We'll go to Grenada, and we'll see the Alhambra," my father explained enthusiastically as we squeezed back into the car. "It's one of the wonders of the world."

If you ask me, a wonder of the world is something natural, like the Grand Canyon, and not just another ruined castle. Anyway, I've never understood what my parents see in ruins. Ruined castles, ruined forts, ruined villages. My parents think that if a building is in good shape, it's not worth seeing.

Spain, it turned out, was an enormous country.

As the hours went by, my brother and I discovered that we had less and less room in the car.

Naturally, I had to push him a little to get more space for myself. And, naturally, he pushed me back.

Then I accidentally sat on his penguin, and he started screaming. My father yelled at both of us. My mother got mad at my father for yelling. My brother blamed me for starting the whole thing. Then I blamed him. Then my father yelled again...

If we were in a comic strip, you would see an old, beat-up car bouncing along a narrow road with smoke coming out of it and a huge balloon hanging over the roof, like this:

Meanwhile, the countryside rolled by. Olive trees, red ground, and boring hills stretching on forever.

"We're in La Mancha now," my mother said happily, as if that meant something to us. "The home of Don Quixote."

"Don who?" my brother asked.

To keep us from fighting, my mother told us the story of Don Quixote, who was a knight in this book by Cervantes, a Spanish writer. The problem with Mr. Quixote was that he was always getting things wrong. He thought that windmills were monsters, and that his old mule was a noble stallion, and that his girlfriend, who was pretty ordinary, was a beautiful princess. Luckily he had a best friend, Sancho Panza, who looked after him.

"I want to read that book," my little brother said.

"When you're older," my father answered. "It's pretty long. Hundreds and hundreds of pages, actually."

"In the meantime, you can just look at the pictures," I told him.

My brother pushed me. And of course I had to push him back, a little harder. Soon we forgot all about Don Quixote, the knight with the sad face. My father tried to break up our fight while keeping one hand on the wheel. My mother yelled at him to keep his eyes on the road.

A typical family trip!

To give everyone a break, we stopped to visit a troglodyte village. Troglodyte, I learned from the guidebook, means someone who lives in a cave, which my father said he would love to do right now, so at least he would have some peace and quiet.

Anyway, in this little town, a long time ago, people moved into caves that the wind and water had hollowed out of the side of a cliff. They are still living there today. They built walls and put in doors and windows.

At first I thought we would see some cavemen. You know, small, hairy people with big jaws and arms hanging down to the ground. But these troglodytes seemed pretty normal. Their caves were modern, with satellite dishes sticking out at all angles from the cliff. That's evolution for you!

Finally, we arrived in the city of Grenada. The problem with that place is that it's up in the mountains, and it got colder and colder as we slowly climbed from the plains up to the city, with our old car huffing and puffing.

Once we got there, for some strange reason my parents decided that we needed to save money.

That's the way they are sometimes. They suddenly decide we're poor, and that we have to squeeze every penny. Usually that happens when we've been traveling for a while.

The way to save money, according to them, was to spend the night in the cheapest, most rundown hotel in the city: La casa de la cucaracha.

That's a joke, of course. Nobody would call their place "The Roach House." The real name of the hotel was El Dorado, which means "The City of Gold." That must have been the owner's idea of a joke.

We went inside to have a look.

"It's so charming," my mother said, admiring the cold marble staircase. "And so authentic."

"Look, all the rooms have a garden view," my father added, pointing to the courtyard full of frozen plants.

"Too bad it's winter," I reminded them.

Maybe my parents thought that a freezing-cold hotel with no heat was charming, but I didn't. All the rooms faced onto an inner patio that was open to the sky, which allowed the cold wind to enter more easily.

"Look!" I said. "We can see the charming patio right through the door."

That's because it had a hole in it the size of a baseball.

"The door doesn't even lock," my brother said suspiciously. He must have been worried that someone would steal his penguin.

No matter how we protested, our parents wouldn't listen. We were doomed to spend the night in the Spanish version of the Ice Hotel.

We were hungry, of course, after a tiring day of fighting in the car. The problem with Spain is that the restaurants don't serve dinner until ten o'clock at night. It's a pretty cruel practice, if you ask me. You could starve to death just waiting for dinner, if you didn't fall asleep first.

Tapas to the rescue!

The same people who came up with the crazy idea of waiting until the middle of the night to eat dinner also invented tapas. They're the things you eat at normal dinner time while you're waiting for ten o'clock to roll around. Makes sense, right?

Tapas are little snacks that are served in all the restaurants and cafés. If you eat enough of them, it's just like dinner.

A lot of people were eating them standing up at the counter, as if they were too much in a hurry to sit down. Not us. We came across a place called El Paraíso del Jamón – The Paradise of Ham. It's not that I'm so crazy about ham, but I wanted to go there. That's because I saw the fireplace. And sure enough, there was a free table right next to it. By that time I was so cold I was just about ready to sit in the fireplace.

We went up to the counter to order. My mother ordered the *conejo* with the *caracoles*. I couldn't believe it. Who would have thought of putting rabbit and snails together in the same dish? But that's exactly what my mother wanted.

My father figured he should outdo her and order something even stranger. So he asked for black rice.

"Why is it black?" my brother wanted to know.

"It's squid ink," I told him. "The squids squirt their ink onto the rice."

"That's gross!" he shouted.

All he would eat was what he called "the brave potatoes." Those were the *patatas bravas*, which was just an ordinary potato salad.

I wanted something really weird to eat, too. So I went for the smoked eels. On the way to Grenada, we'd stopped by a marsh for a picnic, and we saw thousands of them wriggling in the shallow, muddy water. They looked like big greasy snakes having a mud-wrestling match.

My brother swore he'd rather die than eat them, and here they were, on the menu.

"You're ordering that on purpose," he accused me.

Maybe he was right.

I held up a long strip of smoked eel and

dropped it into my mouth. Unfortunately, he wouldn't look at me. The eel tasted, well... smoky. And a little bit eely, too.

I don't think I would order eel again.

Meanwhile, Max ate potatoes and bread. By the time we got back to the hotel, he wasn't feeling that well. It wasn't the potatoes. He had a fever. My mother bundled him up and put him to bed. Meanwhile, my father and I went downstairs to beg for a heater for the room my brother and I shared.

"*Por favór,*" said my father, smiling the biggest smile he could, and holding his high school Spanish book in his hand. "*Queremos una cosa para el calór.*"

Which means, more or less, "Please, we would like a thing for the heat."

I wondered what we'd get. A stove? A book of matches? A sweater?

"*Qué quiere?*" answered the man at the desk. He wasn't smiling at all.

When words fail, try sign language. Which is what my father did. He pouted like a little kid, and put his arms around himself and shivered to show he was freezing. He brushed an imaginary tear from his eye. Then he rubbed his hands together, as if he were trying to warm up.

I was afraid the man at the desk would think he

wanted to start a fire in the room by rubbing two sticks together.

Meanwhile, I went and sat in the darkest corner of the lobby and flipped through a magazine. I pretended very hard that a) I could read Spanish perfectly, and b) that man was not my father.

Finally, Señor Dorado exclaimed, "You want hot!"

"Yes!" my father yelled in return, as if together, he and Señor Dorado had just won the world charades championship.

Señor Dorado disappeared into a back room behind his desk. A minute later he returned and handed my father the world's smallest radiator. My dad proudly marched up the four flights of cold marble stairs and into my brother's room, where he plugged in the machine.

"See?" my father said triumphantly as the little metal coils started to turn red. "All the modern comforts!"

Then the three of us tramped out of the room and left my brother snoring under a mountain of sweaters.

We went back to my parents' room. There, "all the modern comforts" included a single bare bulb hanging on a wire from the ceiling. My mother sat cross-legged in the middle of the bed to read, while my father and I went into the bathroom where the other lightbulb hung. I got to read sitting on the toilet, with the seat down, of course. My father read perched on the edge of the tub.

I was glad I had *Robinson Crusoe* with me. I sure needed to be somewhere else!

Everything was quiet in our little library until my mother saw the cockroaches running along the ceiling right above her head.

"Oh, that's disgusting!" she shrieked.

Then her voice became extremely calm and determined. She turned to me and said, "Go and see how your brother is doing."

"He's sleeping," I said. "He's all right."

"Go make sure he's warm enough."

I knew that tone of voice. It was her your-father-and-I-need-to-talk voice.

And guess what? The next night we stayed in a four-star hotel in the most modern part of town. There was plenty of heat, and not a *cucaracha* in sight. Not to mention the super-satellite TV we had in our room. We watched the Simpsons in French, motorcycle racing in English and a soccer game in Spanish.

I guess we saved enough money on our first night in the Ice Hotel to afford this place.

Oh, I almost forgot. We did end up seeing the Alhambra, the castle that my parents thought was one of the wonders of the world. It wasn't in ruins after all. It was a giant castle built on top of a hill, and it was made out of red stone that glowed at sunset. The best part were the gardens. They were full of fountains and pools with the biggest goldfish I had ever seen. Now this would be a great fishing spot – almost too easy! I couldn't wait to tell Rachid and Ahmed about the size of the fish.

There are about a million rooms in the

Alhambra, and my parents of course wanted to visit all of them. But my brother finally figured out how to get them to leave. He managed to fall into one of the goldfish pools. My father had to fish him out, and he got soaked in the process. Meanwhile, my mother turned bright red.

"I really think it's time to go home, right now!" she declared.

By "home," she meant Celeriac. And I totally agreed!

EIGHT

Encounters of the wooly kind

The year was going by really fast. Already it was spring. I knew I had to make the most of the time that was left.

One of the big spring events around Celeriac is the Fête de la Transhumance. A *transhumance* is like a giant moving day for sheep. Every spring, the sheep all pack up and move to the mountains where it's cooler, and where the grass is greener and tastier.

Of course, they don't do this all by themselves. They have human beings to help them. And those humans think the move is an excellent excuse to have a party.

So one weekend we headed into the mountains in our sardine can on wheels, in search of the party. The mountain roads were steep and winding, and soon my brother started to turn green. I was half-green myself. Our car's engine was barely powerful enough to get us up the hills, and the brakes were just strong enough to keep us from flying over the edge of some cliff because, of course, the narrow country roads don't have guard rails.

"I don't feel so good," my brother complained.

"We're almost there," my father said, trying to sound cheerful.

Almost where? I wondered. We were on a mountain ridge, and though I could see a really long way, there wasn't a village in sight.

We started up another steep hill. I could hear the motor working hard, like in *The Little Engine that Could.*

"Maybe I could get out and push," I suggested.

"My stomach hurts," my brother complained some more.

"Don't you think we should stop?" my mother said to my father.

"We can't, not on a hill like this. We'd roll all the way back down."

"I think I'm going to throw up."

Finally we finished climbing the hill and came to a wide plateau. *Le Plateau de Pisse-Mouton*, the sign read. The Sheep-Pee Plateau — they really know how to name places in France!

"This looks like a good place to stop," my mother said happily.

Not that we had any choice. Suddenly, out of nowhere, we were surrounded by an army of sheep. We had driven right into their moving day. And they weren't following the road. They were going cross-country.

My poor brother! First he couldn't get out of the car because we were trying to climb a mountain. And now he couldn't get out because we were packed in by sheep on all sides.

The windows were open so my brother could get some fresh air. The sheep turned out to be very

nosy. They stuck their heads in the car and bleated loudly.

My mother screamed as a sheep tried to munch on her hair. Quickly, my father rolled up his window. Max tried to close his, but it was too late. One of the sheep made a grab for his penguin. My brother slapped the sheep on the top of its wooly head.

"Baaaah!" the sheep bleated.

My brother started yelling at it. Add the noise of the bells — half the animals were wearing bells around their necks — and you had a real orchestra!

The shepherd came past, walking in the middle of the sea of sheep. He looked exactly like a shepherd out of a book, with a staff, a pipe, a cap over his eyes — and, yes, a sheepskin coat.

"What's the matter with you? What are you doing here?" he asked my father, not very friendly.

"I'm going to the *transhumance*," he told the shepherd.

"Well, you're in it. Up to your eyeballs. The road is closed."

I remembered a sign I'd seen on the way up the hill. *Circulation perturbée*, it read. The circulation is perturbed. Hardly the same thing as "Road Closed for Sheep."

"What do we do now?" my father asked.

"Enjoy the view," barked the shepherd, and he

followed his flock with his dog leading the way. A sheep dog, of course.

"I have to go to the bathroom," my brother announced.

"Go with him, Charlie," my mother said. "But be careful."

What's so dangerous about sheep? you might ask. But when you're penned in on all sides by a sea of bleating, wooly animals that are all in a terrible hurry to get to their meadows covered in delicious, grade-A mountain grass, it feels a little strange. Not to mention the flies that have their moving day at the same time as the sheep.

I pushed open the car door. That wasn't easy. Sheep are heavier than you think.

"Be careful!" my mother said.

Little by little, I was able to get the door all the way open.

"Come on, Max! Follow me, and don't be afraid. Sheep teeth aren't very sharp," I told him, as if I knew all about it.

We fought our way through the river of sheep. We made it to the edge of the road, and my brother watered the grass. Then we sat on a shelf of rock and watched the parade.

Some of the sheep were wearing brightly colored pompons on their heads. Others had decorations painted on their wool — stars, half-moons, letters and other symbols in bright pinks and purples. Those sheep really knew how to dress up for a party!

I found out later that the owners decorated them that way so they could recognize whose sheep were whose. I don't think the sheep had any say in the matter. I can't imagine they would have asked for pink pompons on their heads.

It was the kind of thing my mother would like, I thought to myself. Sure enough, she had her camera out, and she was busy taking pictures of the decorated sheep.

Sometimes she's so predictable!

When the parade was finally over, we walked back to the car.

"Now where do we go?" I asked.

"We'll go where the sheep went. That's where the action is," my father answered.

We had come all this way to go to a sheep festival, so it made sense to follow them and their shepherd.

At the bottom of the mountain that we had worked so hard to climb, there was the figure of a sheep cut out of wood, painted white of course, and an arrow pointing to the Plateau d'Estafette. We had one more hill to climb.

That's where we ran into the biggest open-air picnic I have ever seen.

And guess what was on the menu?

"It doesn't seem fair," I said. "I mean, we're eating their cousins or sisters or neighbors, right in front of them."

Still, I served myself from a plate of lamb chops grilled over an open fire. The decorated sheep ran circles around us, their bells clanging like crazy.

"Do you think they know?" I wondered.

"Of course not." My brother reached for another lamp chop. It was his fourth, but who was counting?

"We don't really know what animals think," my mother said.

I watched the sheep to see if I could tell what they were thinking. Every once in a while one of them would get the idea in its wooly head to go exploring somewhere new. Then, little by little, all the other sheep would follow, even though they didn't know why or where they were going. I think the worst part about being a sheep is that you can never be alone. Wherever you go, all your friends will follow.

After lunch, my father took us on a tour of the Sheep Show. There was a craft fair with sheep cheeses, and sheepskin jackets, and a competition for the best sheep dog. Those dogs were really smart. They could herd sheep through hoops, or even ignore a big bowl of food until they had finished the job. My brother would never be able to get a job as a sheep dog.

We visited a store that sold shepherd clothes and hats, and even wooden staffs. Everything you needed to dress up as a shepherd for Halloween.

"I like sheep better than bulls," my brother said.

"Me, too," my father agreed.

"A sheep will never chase you into a phone booth," I said.

"Very funny," my father told me, glancing nervously at my mother. She still hadn't forgiven us for running with the bulls.

He bought her a present. An antique sheep-bell made out of old rusty metal. The clapper inside the bell was an actual sheep's bone.

My father isn't very good at choosing presents. My mother inspected the rusty bell.

"Gee, thanks," she said.

I could tell she was wondering what she could possibly do with an old metal sheep bell.

After the big picnic, we climbed higher into the mountains on the wind-swept, curving roads that twisted like snakes. By the end of the day, when we got out of the car in a little village, in search of a hotel, we could see our breath. Spring definitely hadn't reached this place yet.

The next morning, we trooped off into the mountains on an expedition, up a steep path that led right from the front door of the hotel. We were the only ones out walking, except for a pair of fishermen who looked like statues at the edge of a lake.

"Just look at the color of that water!" my mother exclaimed. "You could never produce a shade like that with my watercolors."

"Easy, it's the same color as Miro's eyes," said my brother. "You just have to mix a lot of blue with a little green."

"The water is turquoise because of the minerals

in the lake," my father explained. "Those minerals come from the mountains."

Here he goes again, I thought. Another scientific lecture. Sometimes I wish he'd just look at things!

There were wildflowers growing everywhere, as thick as a carpet. My brother picked a little bouquet and gave them to my mother, just to get on her good side. And of course it worked.

Meanwhile, we kept walking. The higher we walked, the colder it got. We had our gym shoes on. They were good for jumping from rock to rock, but my toes were starting to freeze over.

"At the top of the path there's a glacier," my father told us. "That's what the man at the hotel said. Let's see if we can get there."

I had never seen a glacier before, except on television.

"If global warming hasn't melted it," my mother remarked.

"I don't think global warming has gotten this far up," my brother said, shivering.

Down by the lake where the fishermen were, the sun was shining. But as I looked up the path, I saw that we were about to climb straight into a bank of gray, swirling clouds. They were coming down the mountain, straight toward us.

Have you ever heard that expression, "Having

your head in the clouds?" It sounds like fun, right? Well, the next minute I had my head in the clouds and it felt cold, clammy and wet. And scary, too, because you couldn't even see the end of your arm.

"Hey, who turned out the lights?" my brother called.

"I don't know if this is such a good idea," I heard my mother say. "We could get lost."

"Well, there are only two ways," my father tried to reassure her. "Up and down. How could we get lost?"

The clouds turned circles around our heads. My brother and my parents disappeared, though I could still hear their voices. From time to time their blurry shapes would loom up, then fade away.

"We came up here for the view," my mother declared. "Well, I can't see a thing."

"The fog will blow away," my father promised her, "sooner or later."

I tramped along the path, through the puddles and among the boulders. Up ahead, my father started to sing "The Sound of Music." Then he and Max decided to have a yodeling contest.

I don't think that put my mother in a better mood.

"I'm giving this fog one more minute," she announced. "Then we're going back the way we came!"

Suddenly, as if they had heard her, the clouds lifted, carried away on a strong wind. The valley opened up and there we were – facing the glacier. It cascaded down the steep side of a tall mountain and ended in a small lake covered by a thin sheet of ice.

The glacier wasn't as big as the ones you see on TV, complete with giant blocks of ice crashing into the sea. Still, it was pretty cool. The ice was blue-green, the same color as the lake. And we could walk on it, too. It wasn't slippery because it was mixed up with rocks and dirt from the mountain.

We hiked past the glacier. Then we came across wrecked concrete bunkers, pieces of broken cannons and rusty coils of barbed wire. I wasn't expecting to see those kinds of things on the top of a mountain.

"Italy and France used to be at war with each other," my mother explained. "That was a long time ago. These days, you can go from one country to the other without a passport."

And that's exactly what we did. We found a line of stone border markers covered with green moss. On one side of the markers was a cross, and on the other a fleur-de-lys. I sat down on one of the stones.

First I put my feet on the Italian side.

"*Voglio degli spaghetti,*" I said, and I waved my hands in the air.

Then I turned to the French side.

"*Je veux manger des crêpes,*" I said.

"I'm hungry," my brother complained.

Of course he'd say that. He always wants to eat, no matter what country he's in.

"I'll take the spaghetti," my mother decided. "With fennel sausages."

That had my brother running down the mountain like a sheep! All that was missing was the purple pompon.

NINE

A year of good stories

The weather grew warmer by the day, and I discovered all kinds of new things to do, especially when school ended. We went swimming in a river called the Ouvèze, not far from our village. The water came out of the mountains, and it was ice-cold, but there were spots along the river where the rocks formed natural swimming pools. They were covered with slippery green moss, and the sun warmed the water in the pools until it was the same temperature as a bathtub.

The Ouvèze was like an aquatic theme park, only with natural waterslides. It was a lot better than the village swimming pool that smelled like

chlorine. My friends
and I slid from pool to
pool on the slick moss. We
went down the whole river, laughing like crazy
with our feet up in the air, splashing all the way. If
you opened your mouth, you had to be careful
that you didn't swallow a fish. By the time we got
back to the village on our bikes, the backsides of
our shorts were hanging in shreds from sliding on
the rocks.

We went on day-long hikes through the mountains and valleys with Daniel and his parents. Since
his father Didier was a science teacher, he pointed
out all kinds of things along the way. There were
birds that lived in tiny holes in the sides of the
river banks. They were called bee-eaters, and they

flew over from North Africa every summer. They were the only animals that were willing to eat wasps and hornets. They must have stomachs of steel!

. I was happier eating the figs and apricots and kiwis and plums that grew along the river. They were growing there just for us.

We crossed the Pont du Gard. It's part of a Roman aqueduct system. Of course, my father had to give us all a history lesson about the Romans, and how they built bridges called aqueducts to bring water to their cities.

One time we went horseback riding at a horse camp. At first I wasn't too sure.

"You should try it," my mother said. "After all, how many chances do you have to ride a horse in Montreal?"

She was right. We live in a big city full of people and cars and buildings. But in some ways, there was really more to do in a little village like Celeriac.

At the stables, I met a girl named Vanina. She'd been riding horses since she was two. I think she even spoke horse. She taught me not be be afraid of the horses, even if they were way bigger than I was.

The first thing you had to do was act as if you knew exactly what you were doing. That wasn't true in my case. But she showed me how to get the horse to jump over a fence, and once we even went on a moonlight ride.

I still have a photograph of Vanina and me and the horse. I hid it someplace hard to find, so my brother won't get his hands on it.

Remember Dr. Rosalie who fixed my brother's knee on the morning of the flood? She became our friend, mostly through her son Florian, who was our age. That was a good thing, because Max was always banging himself up by jumping off a roof or falling out of a tree. You know, just so we wouldn't forget that he was still around. Every time she stitched up my brother, Dr. Rosalie would make him laugh.

"If I put any more stitches in you, you'll look like Frankenstein!" she told him.

She and her husband decided to organize a going-away party for us. Every single person we knew from the village was there. The party began on a Saturday afternoon. People had set up long tables in Dr. Rosalie's yard – sorry, in her *jardin* – underneath a trellis where vines grew. The tables werc as long as a soccer field. There was room for everyone. Daniel and his family, Rachid, Ahmed, Florian and my whole soccer team, all the men from my father's team, everyone who had ever taken my mother's art classes, the goat-cheese lady, Marco the grocer, Carpini the baker. Madame Mendes and her husband even brought Linda in a wheelbarrow. And of course Vanina was there.

I ncver realized I had made so many friends in such a short time.

Two lambs were roasting over a low fire. Someone had driven down to a fishing port on the coast and come back with a whole box of sardines. There were pies made of onions and wild asparagus no bigger than a baby's finger, and salads made from grcens that someone had gathered in the woods. There were goat cheeses that smelled so strong I thought they would just get up and walk away.

And, of course, because we were in Celeriac, the land of grapes, there were barrels of wine.

Whenever you put wine and adults together, there's bound to be some foolishness. Daniel's father took some bottles of Champagne from the freezer, then pulled out a scimitar, which is the kind of curved sword a pirate might use.

Didier was going to show us how to open bottles without removing the corks.

Before I knew it, the tops of the bottles were flying through the air like unguided missiles. My brother and I hit the dirt. The jagged glass rockets flew over our heads and stuck into the sides of trees.

Strangely enough, that didn't seem to bother anyone else, even my mother who was always telling us to be careful.

After it was finally safe to stand up again, Marco asked us what we would remember most about our year in the village. What stories would we tell our friends back in Montreal?

"The bull story!" my brother burst out. "When my father got trapped in the phone booth."

Everyone started laughing, including my father. What else could he do?

"What about you?" Marco asked me.

"The flood," I told him. "When Monsieur Carpini and Monsieur Soulier rowed their boat down our street."

"What about the snowstorm of the century?" Marco asked.

I laughed. Of course, the Great Celeriac Blizzard. Were there howling winds and freezing temperatures, with snow drifts piling up to the windowledge? Not exactly. We had one inch of watery snow.

"Remember that day, Madame Mendes?" I asked her. "You told us to go back into our house before we froze to death. And you wouldn't even let Linda go outside."

"I remember something about that day," Daniel's father said to me.

I knew exactly what he was talking about.

"I was just trying to have some fun the way we do back home," I tried to explain. "So I threw a couple of snowballs at Rachid…"

"Unfortunately, he missed," Daniel's father continued, "and he hit me instead!"

"That was a little embarrassing," I admitted.

"And do you know what this whipper-snapper told me after he hit me in the head with two snowballs?" Daniel's father asked everyone at the table.

"I kind of forget," I said in a very small voice.

"But, *monsieur*, snowballs are a Canadian tradition," he said, imitating me in a scared, squeaky voice.

"What did you do then?" my mom asked.

"I threw them right back," Daniel's father said.

"Yeah," I complained, laughing the whole time. "And he hit me, too, with both of them!"

My story was a big success. It was almost as good as the one about my father getting trapped in the phone booth. For all I know, people are still telling the snowball story back in Celeriac!

"So, *mon garçon*, you liked it here?" Marco asked me.

"You bet!"

"*Alors*, then you must come back."

I promised him I would. And I promised myself, too.

My checklist

On our last morning in Celeriac, Daniel's father came to drive us to the train station. Fortunately, our sardine-can car was staying behind. That was one thing I wouldn't miss.

Rachid and Ahmed were hanging around the square, but they weren't playing soccer. They were watching us pack. They looked sad.

I felt a little embarrassed. I don't know why. Maybe because I was moving on to another world, far from here, and they were staying behind.

Rachid came up to me.

"How about a trade?" he asked.

At first I was confused. Then I understood. He

was wearing a green and red soccer jersey from the Moroccan national team. I was wearing my old Montreal Expos T-shirt.

I pulled it off and gave it to him, and he did the same. Then we both put on each other's shirts, just like the pros do after a game.

"I'll be back," I told Rachid and Ahmed.

"We'll be here," they said.

As I was stowing the last of our bags in the car, my mother asked me, "Do you still have your list?"

"What list?"

"The list of things you wanted to see in Paris."

"How come?"

"Because that's where we're going."

For once we were going some place I wanted to go. Amazing! You'd better believe I still had that list. It was at the bottom of my suitcase, but I hadn't forgotten what was on it.

Daniel's father started up the car.

"Let's go. Unless you want to miss your train."

Part of me wanted to stay. Part of me wanted to go. I guess that's the way it is with traveling. You discover a new place. At first it's not easy. Then you learn how to live there, and you make new friends. But then it's time to leave again...

Of course, going to Paris wasn't bad either. We

traveled there on one of the fastest trains in the world. It goes more than 300 kilometers an hour! The cows rushed by like black-and-white blurs, and the trees morphed into speeding broccoli. We went from our little village to Paris in three and a half hours, and I didn't even get jet lag.

The first thing on my list was the Eiffel Tower. You can see it from nearly anywhere in Paris, and from a distance it looks like a toy. But when you climb to the very top, you can look down and see millions of people scurry-ing around like ants. And the traffic jams — they're incredible!

After Celeriac, Paris was so huge. Max said he could see every flowerpot on every balcony in the city, and every Frenchman wearing a beret and carrying a baguette. But, as usual, he was exaggerating.

Of course, my father had to give us another one of his his-tory lessons. He pointed out the Arc de

Triomphe, and told us how Napoleon had put it up in the nineteenth century to celebrate one of his victories. He showed us where the Bastille had been, which was a prison that was destroyed in the French Revolution. The people attacked it and tore it apart, brick by brick. All that's left is a column with a statue on top.

Imagine dark passageways with the walls and ceiling made out of human bones. That's what the Catacombs are like, where the Romans buried their dead. Things got extra scary when I accidentally dropped my candle, and it went out. There I was, in the dark, surrounded by skeletons. Suddenly I was afraid to move. But then Max came around the corner from another passageway, with his candle. I was pretty happy to see him.

Instead of taking a ride on the Seine river in a tourist boat, we cruised through the Paris sewers. They were smelly, all right, just the way they were supposed to be. In fact, they were worse than the cheese lady's oldest goat cheese. During the Second World War, people used the sewers to hide out in and have secret meetings. But this time, believe it or not, I saw a crew making a movie down there.

When we got to Notre Dame church, the line to go up in the towers was so long that we gave up. Sometimes there are too many people in Paris. Luckily, my mother had brought along her binoculars, so we took turns looking at the gargoyles hanging by their claws from the edge of the cathedral. Max didn't want to look at them. He said they would give him nightmares. I reminded him that they were there to chase away the evil spirits by being even scarier than they were. So they were just doing their job.

I finally got back home. But I can still remember everything that happened in our speck-of-dust village, from the duck thief to Rachid's going-away present that I'm wearing right now.

I think I'd like to stay in one place for a while. But when it's time to go traveling again, I'll be ready...

THE END